BoBo Loses His Glasses

A BoBo Book

AuthorHouse™
1663 Liberty Drive
Bloomington, IN 47403
www.authorhouse.com
Phone: 1 (800) 839-8640

Published by AuthorHouse 07/10/2019

ISBN: 978-1-7283-1603-1 (sc)
ISBN: 978-1-7283-1602-4 (hc)
ISBN: 978-1-7283-1604-8 (e)

Library of Congress Control Number: 2019907791

Print information available on the last page.

authorHOUSE®

This is a story about our grandpa.

He may be different from your grandpa but he <u>always</u> makes us feel special.

We call him BoBo.

For my family, who has always helped me find myself when lost.
– M.B.

For David, my many nieces and nephews, as
well as my great nieces and nephews.
– D.W.

BoBo Loses His Glasses

A BoBo BooK

Megan Burton

Illustrated by Dominic Wolocko

Hi!

My name is Lizzie and this is my brother, Alex.

While most people have a grandpa to visit, we have BoBo.

It was a sunny morning as we walked over to BoBo's house.
When we got there, the door was slightly open.
"BoBo? Are you home?" we called.

Should we push the door open and walk inside the house? Or should we ring the doorbell?

If you want to push the door open and go in the house, turn to page 6.
If you want to ring BoBo's doorbell and wait on the porch, jump to page 8.

"BoBo!" we yelled as we walked through the doorway.

Just then, BoBo came stumbling toward us. There was something different about BoBo today. BoBo was NOT walking straight. Each time he took a step he bumped into something, like a wall or piece of furniture.

"Watch out!" we yelled as BoBo bumped into Grammy's favorite lamp!

Turn to page **10**.

"DING! DONG!" rang the doorbell.
No one answered.

"DING! DONG!" the bell rang again.

Suddenly, strange noises came from inside the house...

The door swung wide open and inside we could see BoBo. We also saw Grammy's favorite lamp broken in pieces on the floor. What a mess!

"BoBo, what is going on?" we asked.

"Well…" he started to say,
"I just cannot seem to find my glasses today and
I need them to see clearly.

Would you please help me look?"

"Here we go!" I said. "Where, oh where, are BoBo's glasses?"

Should we start looking in the kitchen or the backyard?

To look in the kitchen, turn to page 12.
To look in the backyard, jump to page 18.

In the kitchen, we looked for BoBo's glasses inside all of the cabinets. We even looked inside the dishwasher! We found a lot of dishes and dirty spoons. We even found BoBo's favorite cookies, but no glasses.

Where should we look next? Should we look in the bedroom or the bathroom?

To look in the bedroom, turn to page 14.

To look in the bathroom, jump to page 16.

In BoBo's bedroom, we looked everywhere! His glasses were not on his pillow. They were not in any drawers and they were definitely not under the bed.

We did find some polka dotted underwear and BoBo's missing bunny slippers though!

Should we look in the bathroom or the backyard next?

To look in the bathroom, turn to page 16.
To look in the backyard, jump to page 18.

When we got to the bathroom, the first place we checked was in the toilet. No glasses in the toilet... thank goodness! No glasses in the sink. No glasses by the toothbrushes.

Where, oh where, are BoBo's glasses?

Where should we look next,
in the family room or the closet?

To look in the family room, jump to page 20.
To look in the closet, jump to page 22.

As we walked outside, BoBo got an idea.

"Maybe I dropped my glasses while I was watering the flowers," he said.

We looked through the flowerbeds in Grammy's garden but BoBo's glasses were not there.

However, we did find a little chipmunk, two worms, and a blue bird taking a bath!

Do you think BoBo's glasses are in the kitchen or the family room?

To look in the kitchen, jump back to page 12.
To look in the family room, turn to page 20.

In the family room, we carefully looked behind the TV and under each couch cushion. We did not find BoBo's glasses but we did find his favorite book, a cowboy hat, Grammy's necklace, and two lollipops.

Where, oh where, are BoBo's glasses?

Should we look in the kitchen or the closet next?

To look in the kitchen, jump back to page 12.

To look in the closet, turn to page 22.

21

Inside the closet, we looked up high on the shelves and we looked down low near the floor. BoBo thought the broom looked like a friend of his and started talking to it.

"Hello. Have you seen my glasses?" he asked.
But a broom can't talk. BoBo really cannot see without his glasses!

Where, oh where, are BoBo's glasses?

We sat down on the front porch. Even though we had searched all over the house, BoBo's glasses were still missing.

We saw a car driving toward the house.

"Well, that must be Grammy," said BoBo. "I will have to tell her I just don't know where I put my glasses."

BoBo stood up. He put his hands in his pockets...

Suddenly, BoBo stopped. "I FOUND THEM!" he yelled as he jumped high into the air.

When BoBo put his glasses on he could see much better.

In fact, he could now see that the car driving toward the house was not Grammy's car at all...

it was an ice cream truck!
"My treat!" yelled BoBo excitedly.

"Now, where did I leave my wallet?"

Where did you help BoBo look?

27

Megan Burton got the inspiration for the BoBo Book Series while watching her father transition into the role of a fun-loving grandpa. The combination of growing up with an overly active imagination and influence from her father's unique sense of humor has encouraged her to write and share her sense of adventure for others to enjoy. Megan and her husband live in Michigan with their two energetic children who take them on adventures daily.

Dominic Wolocko is an accomplished artist having graduated with a BFA from Philadelphia College of Art with Honors. With over 30 years of experience, his illustrations have been published in the Philadelphia Inquirer, the Philadelphia Daily News, the Baltimore Sun, Science Digest, and Philadelphia Magazine. Dominic is a Detroit native currently living in Philadelphia with his husband. His family, consisting of 6 siblings, 13 nephews and nieces, and 20 great nephews and nieces, receive personally drawn Christmas cards every year.

The character BoBo is based on Megan's father. Dominic is also Megan's uncle and BoBo's brother.

Look for more adventures with BoBo!